JUSTINE McKEEN
vs. the QUEEN of MEAN

JUSTINE McKEEN
vs. the QUEEN of MEAN

Sigmund Brouwer
illustrated by Dave Whamond

ORCA BOOK PUBLISHERS

Library and Archives Canada Cataloguing in Publication

Brouwer, Sigmund, 1959-, author
Justine McKeen vs. the queen of mean / Sigmund Brouwer;
illustrated by Dave Whamond.
(Orca echoes)

Issued in print and electronic formats.
ISBN 978-1-4598-0397-8 (pbk.).--ISBN 978-1-4598-0398-5 (pdf).--
ISBN 978-1-4598-0399-2 (epub)

I. Whamond, Dave, illustrator II. Title. III. Series: Orca echoes
PS8553.R68467J883 2014   jc813'.54   C2014-901956-4
C2014-901957-2

First published in the United States, 2014
Library of Congress Control Number: 2014936072

Summary: Justine is faced with the challenge of convincing the Queen of Mean
that being environmentally conscious is worthwhile.

Orca Book Publishers gratefully acknowledges the support for its publishing programs
provided by the following agencies: the Government of Canada through the Canada Book
Fund and the Canada Council for the Arts, and the Province of British Columbia
through the BC Arts Council and the Book Publishing Tax Credit.

*Orca Book Publishers is dedicated to preserving the environment and has printed
this book on Forest Stewardship Council® certified paper.*

Cover artwork and interior illustrations by Dave Whamond
Author photo by Reba Baskett

ORCA BOOK PUBLISHERS   ORCA BOOK PUBLISHERS
PO Box 5626, Stn. B   PO Box 468
Victoria, BC Canada   Custer, WA USA
v8R 6s4   98240-0468

www.orcabook.com
Printed and bound in Canada.

17 16 15 14 • 4 3 2 1

To the Savannah in my life who inspired this story.
(And who is NOT mean in any way!)

Chapter One

Justine stood at her desk and looked down at the list in her hand. She opened her mouth to speak, but the next noise did not come from her throat. Instead, it came from her friend Michael, who sat in the middle row.

"Snake!" Michael screamed from the middle row. He jumped up from his desk. "Snake!"

Justine had expected that. Just not at this moment. After all, Michael was supposed to be paying attention, not opening his desk.

All of the other students were staring at Michael instead of waiting for Justine to talk about Earth Day and what they could do to help the environment.

"Please tell me it's a rubber snake," said Mrs. Howie from behind her desk. "Remember, this *is* the first day of April."

Mrs. Howie had short brown hair, thick glasses and a very nice smile. She was Justine's favorite teacher.

Michael went back to his desk and opened the lid and looked inside. "Yes," he said. "It's a rubber snake tied to a string. The string was tied to my desk top, so when I opened the desk, the snake jumped out at me."

A few of the students giggled. One of them laughed very hard. This was Safdar, another one of Justine's close friends.

"You sounded like a little kid!" Safdar said. He held his stomach because he was laughing so hard. "Who would fall for something like that?"

"Did you put the snake there?" Mrs. Howie asked Safdar. "That was a great April Fool's joke."

"No," Safdar said. "I didn't."

Safdar was telling the truth. Justine knew that before school started, Jimmy Blatzo had snuck into the classroom and put the snake in Michael's desk as an April Fool's trick. Blatzo was one of the older students in the school. He was a friend of Justine, Michael and Safdar.

"What a shame," Mrs. Howie said to Safdar. She pointed to the apple on her desk. "It was a much better joke than switching my apple for one with half a gummy worm sticking out the side. That's an old trick. It didn't fool me for a second."

Mrs. Howie bit into the apple. She chewed and swallowed, then smiled at the class. When she put the apple down, the worm was gone.

Justine didn't want to tell Mrs. Howie that maybe she needed new glasses. Justine had definitely seen the worm move as she walked into class.

Mrs. Howie waited for the students to settle down again.

"Justine," she said, "we are ready."

"Thank you," Justine said. She looked at the students. "On April 22, it will be Earth Day. That

means we have only three weeks to complete a project to help our planet."

She saw that Safdar was not listening. Safdar already knew what Justine was going to suggest, because Safdar had helped her come up with the list. So had Michael.

Justine paused, because she saw that Safdar was about to look inside his desk for something. Just as she expected, a second later Safdar jumped up and screamed.

"Let me guess," Mrs. Howie said. "A snake? Tied to a string?"

Justine knew that Blatzo was going to find all of this funny. But she wanted to get through her list. So after Michael stopped laughing and Safdar sat down again, Justine was finally able to ask for help.

"Okay," Justine said, moving to the front of the class. "We need student volunteers to go into the woods with me and do some species counts. You can choose flower buds, frogs, spiders or ants."

"Wow," the new girl said, rolling her eyes. "If this is an April Fool's trick, it's the worst one in the history of the world." The new girl's name was Savannah Blue. It was her first day of class.

"Pardon me?" Justine said.

Savannah laughed. "Nice try. What kind of idiot would want to count spiders or frogs or ants?"

Chapter Two

Mrs. Howie cleared her throat. It wasn't because she needed to cough. It was more like a warning. All of the students knew this. But Savannah Blue had just moved to the school. She didn't know it.

"And those clothes," Savannah said. "Did someone play an April Fool's trick on you?"

Justine was proud of how she looked. Today, it was purples and greens. She also had a nice hat on, with a frog emblem stitched on the side.

Mrs. Howie cleared her throat again. "Savannah, one of the rules in our classroom is that we don't say mean things."

"Oh," Savannah said. "I'm sorry. Justine actually *likes* to dress like that?"

"She's the Queen of Green," Michael said. "She buys her clothes at secondhand stores because that's a way to reuse clothing."

"And she's had lots of great projects to help the environment," Safdar explained. "We built a greenhouse out of soda bottles once. And we started the walking school bus and—"

"So," Savannah said, "she's the reason I had to walk to school today? Nice."

By her tone of voice, everyone knew Savannah did *not* think it was nice to walk to school.

"Because of Justine," a girl named Sydney said, "they put decals on our school windows to save birds from flying into the glass."

"We all save uneaten food from the cafeteria, plus we started a project of cleaning up dog poop at the park. All thanks to Justine," Michael added.

"Wow," Savannah said. "Saving uneaten food and cleaning up dog poop. Where do I sign up?"

Mrs. Howie cleared her throat. "Also, Savannah, we don't like sarcasm in our classroom. Sarcasm is often mean."

"I'm not asking this sarcastically," Savannah said. "But why would I want to sign up to count frogs or ants?"

Everyone in the class looked at Justine, waiting for her to answer. After all, Justine *was* the Queen of Green.

"It's for national science projects," Justine answered. "Real scientists use information like this from across the country to see what is happening in the environment."

"Why does it matter?" Savannah asked. "And I promise, that is not a sarcastic question. I really want to know."

"Well," Justine said, "if the numbers drop, it shows that the environment is being hurt in a local area. Once we know that, we can take steps to help."

"But why should I care?" Savannah asked. "It's just bugs and frogs."

"Because we should all care about our planet," Justine said. "It's important to be green."

"My dad says people who make a big show about being green are just looking for attention," Savannah answered. "I don't need that kind of attention. Do you? Is that why you like everyone to call you the Queen of Green? Is that why you make sure everyone knows you buy secondhand clothes? Because you want us to think you care more about the environment than we do? So you can think you are better than people who aren't green?"

"Well…" Justine, for once, didn't have an answer.

"I'm happy with my life," Savannah said. "I don't care about frogs or bugs, so if you can't give me a good reason why I should care, then I won't sign up to be a volunteer."

Mrs. Howie stood up behind her desk. Everyone in the classroom knew this was not a good sign.

"It seems," Mrs. Howie said, "that Justine and Savannah have a new assignment to work on together. On Earth Day, the two of them will report to the class on why it matters to care about the environment."

Chapter Three

At lunch, Savannah Blue walked toward the table where Justine was eating lunch with her friends Michael, Safdar and Jimmy Blatzo. Savannah had a glass of water in each hand.

"That's Savannah Blue," Safdar said to Blatzo.

"We were just talking about you," Michael said to Savannah.

"What's your name?" Savannah asked Blatzo.

"Jimmy Blatzo." Blatzo stood up. He was very big. He crossed his arms and frowned at Savannah as he looked down on her. He spoke in his deepest voice. "I heard you gave Justine a rough time in class."

"Is that the best you can do, Blatzo?" Savannah said. "A mean look and crossed arms? I'm soooo terrified."

"Only Justine calls me Blatzo," he growled.

"Blatzo," Savannah said. "You have lettuce in your teeth. It makes you look silly. How about you sit down?"

"Huh?" Blatzo ran a tongue across his teeth.

"You're not sitting," Savannah said. She reached up and pressed on his shoulders and made him sit. "That's better, Blatzo."

Savannah sat at the table beside Justine. She looked at Michael, Safdar and Blatzo. All three frowned at her.

"My," Savannah said. "Aren't I the popular one."

"Maybe you should find someplace else to sit," Safdar said. "Right, Jimmy?"

Blatzo was still checking his teeth for lettuce.

"It's okay," Justine said. "I remember what it was like to be the new girl in school. It would be great if Savannah joined us for lunch."

"After how she tried to make you look bad in class?" Michael asked.

15

"I won't sit here for long," Savannah said. "I don't like hanging out with losers. I just want to get something straight with the Queen of Green. What a stupid name."

"Better the Queen of Green than the Queen of Mean," Michael said.

"Hey," Savannah said. "I like that. My first day at school and already I have a nickname."

"Grrr," Blatzo said.

"Stay in your cage, Blatzo," Savannah said. "This will be quick. I have a simple bet for the Queen of Green."

"I'm not really the betting kind," Justine said.

"Well, you're the one who got me dragged into a stupid bug and frog count. So you're going to give me a chance to get out of doing the report. Unless you are afraid of a challenge."

"It's not that I'm afraid…" Justine said.

"I'll do it," Blatzo said. "I'll take the challenge for Justine. What is it?"

Chapter Four

"The challenge is simple," Savannah said. "If you can balance a full glass of water on the back of each of your hands and not spill a drop, without help from anyone, I'll do all the work on the report. If you spill or ask for help, then Justine does all the bug and frog counting that I was supposed to do. And she writes the report for the presentation on Earth Day that she and I are supposed to do together."

"We're supposed to take video," Michael said. "You have to be in the video when we are in the woods."

"Fine," Savannah said. "I'll take my iPad and sit under a tree and play *Minecraft* while you guys do the work. Stupid bug and frog count."

"Only if you win the challenge," Blatzo said. "I'm an athlete. I can balance a glass of water on the back of each of my hands."

"You can't spill a drop," Savannah said. "And nobody can help you. Remember, those are the conditions."

"And if I balance without spilling a drop," Blatzo said, "not only do you do the report and the bug count, but you stop being the Queen of Mean. Those are my conditions."

"Blatzo, you don't need to do this," Justine said. "If Savannah doesn't want to write the report or do a bug or frog count, I'm okay with that. I'll do her work."

"Don't talk like that," Blatzo said. "The Queen of Mean is going down. Unless she's afraid of the bet."

"Deal," Savannah said. "You balance the glasses on your hands. Nobody helps you. If you don't spill any water, I'll do the report and stop being mean. That would be a shame though. I really like the name. It has a nice ring to it. The Queen of Mean."

"Fine, let's do this," Blatzo said.

"Put your hands on the table. Palms down," Savannah said.

Blatzo did. Savannah placed a nearly full glass of water on the back of Blatzo's right hand. Then the back of his left hand.

"See?" Blatzo said. "Done. Not a drop of water spilled."

"Remember," Savannah said. "You can't spill a drop. And nobody can help you."

"Look close," Blatzo said. "Not even a wobble. You could add more water to each glass and I still wouldn't spill a drop. I told you. I'm an athlete."

"Not even a wobble," Savannah said. "Very good, Blatzo."

"Now what?" he asked.

"Nothing," Savannah answered. "There wasn't a time limit on the bet. Make sure you stay nice and steady."

The bell rang. Students got up from the tables around them to go to class.

Justine, Safdar and Michael stood. So did Savannah.

Blatzo stayed at the table, looking at a glass of water on each of his hands.

"Hey," Blatzo said. "I have to go to class too."

"Good luck," Savannah said. "Nobody is allowed to help, remember? I'll be very impressed if you can take your hands off the table without spilling any water. And I think class starts in about two minutes."

Blatzo stared at the glasses of water on the backs of his hands.

Then he groaned and, in frustration, banged his forehead on the table between his hands. He didn't spill a drop. He was an athlete.

"Yup," Savannah said with satisfaction. "I *am* the Queen of Mean. Great name. Very cool. Think it will look good on a T-shirt?"

Chapter Five

After school, Michael, Safdar and Jimmy Blatzo met with Justine at their usual place, the flagpole in front of the school.

"I have an idea for how to get back at Savannah," Safdar said. "Tomorrow, when we head into the woods for the project, we should play a trick on her."

"That would be good," Michael said. "Right, Jimmy? We could get her back for tricking you with the water."

"I like playing tricks," Blatzo said. "After all, I did make you guys scream with my April Fool's snakes in your desks. But..."

Blatzo stopped for a second. "I have to admit, Savannah did impress me with the water-glass stunt.

Don't get mad at me for saying this, but I think maybe I could even like her as a friend."

"What?" Safdar said. "You should have heard what she said to Justine!"

"I heard," Blatzo answered. "About twenty times already. But Savannah kinda reminds me of someone else that I like."

Blatzo pointed at Justine. Justine didn't notice. She was staring at her shoes.

"Well," Safdar said, "if Savannah isn't going to help with the project, I still think we need to make her pay."

"Yeah," Michael said. "What's your idea?"

"We'll pretend to eat deer poop! That will gross her out and we can have the last laugh."

Michael gave Safdar a high five. "Great idea!"

Then Michael paused. "Um, how do we do that?"

"Easy," Safdar said. "I'll walk ahead of you guys in the woods. I'll drop some chocolate-covered raisins on the ground at the spot where we are supposed

to meet. When you guys get there, one of you picks up some of the raisins and eats them."

"I'll do it," Michael said. He paused. "Um, how do you know that deer poop looks like chocolate-covered raisins?"

"While we were in the library today, I looked it up online," Safdar said. "You can hardly tell the difference—at least, not by looking at it. Now moose poop, on the other hand, is a totally different thing. It looked like you could fill a bucket with moose poop."

"That is a great idea," Michael said. "I'm in." He looked over at Justine. "And maybe it will put a smile back on her face."

Chapter Six

The next day after school, Justine led the way down a path through the woods. The hill was steep, and at the bottom was a marshy area.

"Frogs and toads are very important to the wetlands," Justine explained as they walked. "They are predators who eat lots of bugs. But they are also prey for animals like herons, lizards, snakes, fish and even bigger frogs."

"Ewww," said Savannah. She was carrying her iPad at the end of the line. Michael and Jimmy Blatzo were in the middle. Safdar had run ahead earlier. He was going to drop chocolate-covered raisins on the ground at the meeting spot under a large tree. "I don't know what's grosser. Eating bugs

or eating frogs. Give me a chocolate milkshake any day."

"Flies eat milkshakes," Justine said.

"Really?" Savannah sounded interested.

"Really?" Blatzo said. "I didn't know that."

"Flies don't have teeth," Justine said. "So if they want to eat sugar, they throw up on the sugar to make it a liquid. Then they suck up the mess that has melted in the sugar. That's like a milkshake, right?"

"You are disgusting," Savannah told Justine. "If I wasn't afraid of getting lost, I'd make sure I stayed so far back that I couldn't hear a word you said."

"Maybe Safdar is lost," Michael said. "I haven't seen him in a while. But I'm not worried. He'll show up. He knows where to meet us."

Michael chuckled, like he was thinking of how he was going to gross out Savannah even more.

"Like I care," Savannah said. "Just get me to a place where I can sit and wait for this to be over."

"Tell me more about frogs," Blatzo said to Justine. He wore one of his *Bird Nerd* T-shirts. He had been given the nickname after rescuing some birds.

"When frog populations drop," Justine said, "it tells scientists that things are going wrong. Like too much ultraviolet light getting into the atmosphere because of air pollution. Or too many pesticides from agriculture. Scientists can use our help tallying frog numbers to track what's happening."

"How do you look for them?" Blatzo asked. "It seems like my job of counting flower buds is a lot easier."

"It's easier to listen for frogs than look for them," Justine answered. "Frogs are experts at hiding, and as long as I don't step into the swampy areas, it will be safe."

"Right," Savannah said. "Like we can tell the difference between types of frogs just by listening."

"I went to a training session at the zoo," Justine said. "It's part of something called Frogwatch. It was very helpful."

"Wasted time," Savannah said. "You could have been playing *Minecraft*. Let me tell you, that's something worth doing."

"Don't worry," Justine said. She stopped. "I get the hint. Here's a spot where you can sit and play on your iPad. We won't make you help us find frogs. Or spiders. Or flower buds. After all, you did win the challenge with Blatzo."

"Look!" Michael said. He pointed at some dark pellets on the ground. "Deer poop!"

"Ewww," Savannah said. "Deer poop! We are walking through a toilet. In fact, the whole woods is just a big toilet for all the animals. Really, we should just go back to a place that has a television. And air-conditioning."

"Are you sure it's deer poop?" Blatzo asked Michael. Just like they had planned.

"Only one way to find out if it's deer poop," Michael said. He reached down and grabbed a few of the dark pellets. "You taste them."

30

He popped them in his mouth.

Then his eyes grew very wide, and he began to spit and spit.

That's when Safdar stepped out from some bushes.

"Hey, guys," Safdar said. "I heard voices so I came back here. But aren't we supposed to be meeting up ahead farther? I've been waiting for you."

Michael couldn't speak. He was too busy spitting and coughing and wiping his tongue with his hands.

"Hey," Safdar said. "What's the matter with him?"

Blatzo pointed at the dark pellets on the ground. Blatzo said, "He ate some of those."

"Those?" Safdar said. "Those?"

Safdar took a closer look.

"Wow," Safdar said. "So that's what deer poop looks like in real life. I guess I went to the wrong spot."

That's when Michael screamed and began to chase him.

Chapter Seven

Justine and Safdar found a fallen log near the edge of the swamp. It was a comfortable place to sit in the shadows of the tall trees.

"Michael and Jimmy have the easy job," Safdar said. "They've even got an app for what they are doing. All they need to do is take photos of flower and tree buds."

"It sure helps scientists," Justine said. "They need to know when and where plants are flowering so they can have a better idea of climate change. It's great if they can get thousands of observations from all across the country."

"I know, I know," Safdar said. "Same with spiders. But flowers are so easy to find. Spiders can just disappear."

"Well," Justine answered, "if it helps, when you are outside, there is always a spider within six feet of you. Indoors, there's always a spider hidden within ten feet."

Safdar stood and dusted off his pants. "Really?"

"Just look around. Your iPod is a perfect camera. Take photos and count. We'll sort out the report in the classroom before we pass it along to the scientists."

Safdar got on his knees and carefully looked under the log. Then he pushed aside some branches of a nearby bush.

"You are being very quiet," he said to Justine.

"I am listening for frogs."

"No," Safdar said. "Quiet like upset. I understand. Savannah really is the Queen of Mean. And it seems like she's trying to make you look bad."

"My grammy said sometimes when people are mean, it's because they aren't getting enough attention,"

Justine said. "They really just want someone to be a friend. So if she ever lets me, I'll try to be a friend."

"Oh," Safdar said. "That's why you haven't tried to fight back."

"Eating deer poop didn't seem like a good plan, I can tell you that," she answered.

Safdar was lifting another branch. He stopped. "Michael will get over being mad at me, right?"

"We *are* in the woods," Justine said. "Anybody could have made the same mistake and put the chocolate-covered raisins in the wrong spot."

"Plus," Safdar said, "you'd think he would have looked more closely before putting them in his mouth. Right?"

Justine didn't answer. She stared ahead as though she was thinking about something else.

"Right?" Safdar said. "Right?"

"What if Savannah is right?" Justine said. "What if I'm the Queen of Green for the same reason that she's the Queen of Mean? So that I can tell myself

I'm more special than other people. Because it makes me feel good about myself."

"What's wrong with that?" Safdar asked. "People should feel good about themselves."

"But I couldn't even give a good reason why we should care about the environment," Justine said. She peered into a bush as she spoke. "Savannah could be right. In our daily lives, being green doesn't seem to make a difference. So why *should* we care?"

Justine waited for Safdar to answer.

"Safdar?" she said. "Safdar?"

She looked over. Safdar had crawled halfway into another bush.

"Take a look at this," Safdar said from inside the bush. "Have you ever watched a spider spin a web? It is so cool."

Justine knelt beside him as he took a closeup video of the spider with his iPod. The beginning of the web stretched from the tip of one branch to another.

"Wow," Justine said. "That *is* really cool."

Both of them forgot all about Savannah as they spent the next twenty minutes watching the spider.

Chapter Eight

Blatzo, Michael, Justine and Safdar arrived at the fallen log they had agreed to meet at before going back to find Savannah.

"Unbelievable," Blatzo said. He grinned from ear to ear. "As we were counting flower buds, we found a fawn. It was so little. It didn't move, it just curled up on the ground. I took video on my phone."

"I googled baby fawns," Michael said. He was just as proud as Blatzo. "Apparently, the mother deer leaves it there while she looks for food. I also read that you shouldn't touch a fawn."

"I've heard people say it's because the mother will reject the baby if it smells like a human," Blatzo said. "But that's not true. It's just that if the mother senses a predator has been nearby, it takes a lot longer for her to return."

As they walked along the path, Blatzo showed the video to Safdar and Justine.

"Wow!" Safdar said. "And you should see the spider web on my iPod."

Blatzo and Michael watched.

"Cooler than a video game!" Michael said. "Savannah doesn't know what she's missing."

"Speaking of Savannah," Justine said as they kept walking, "look ahead. She's up in the tree, pretending she doesn't see us."

"She's probably trying to play another trick on us," Blatzo said. "Like dropping something on our heads. What should we do?"

"I have an idea," Justine said. She explained it to Blatzo, Michael and Safdar.

"You sure you want to do that?" Michael asked.

"Yeah," Safdar said. "She doesn't deserve something like that."

"Brilliant," Blatzo said. "Let's do it."

Blatzo looked at Michael and Safdar.

"Yes," Michael said. "Brilliant."

"I like it," Safdar said. "Let's do it."

When they reached the base of the tree, Justine said, "Hey, where's Savannah?"

"I hope she's okay," Blatzo said. "I like her a lot. I wouldn't want her to be lost."

"Yeah," Safdar said. "I like her too. She makes me laugh."

"I'm glad she moved to our school," Michael said. "I hope she'll sit with us at lunch tomorrow."

"You guys are right," Justine said. "It would be nice if she became a friend."

From a branch above them, Savannah said, "You guys are idiots. You think I don't know that you know I'm up here?"

"Well," Justine said, "it was worth a try. Really, it would be great if we were friends. You're the person who helped me answer an important question."

"I don't really care," Savannah said. "I'm too busy up here. You should see the nest in the branch below me. It has five little birds, and every time the mother shows up with a worm, they make a lot of noise and pop their mouths wide-open. It's the coolest thing. I've been taking video on my iPad."

Chapter Nine

Justine, Michael, Safdar and Blatzo watched Savannah begin to climb down the tree. When she was near the bottom, she said to Justine, "Can you help me with this?"

"Yes," Justine said.

Savannah reached down and handed her iPad to Justine. Savannah held the bottom branch with both hands. She swung down. There were twigs in her hair and stains on her pants and shirt.

"There's something on your back," Justine said. "Let me get it for you."

Justine reached across and brushed an ant off Savannah's back.

"Thanks," Savannah said. "Up in the tree, I didn't want to move because I wanted the mother bird to keep coming back. There were ants everywhere. Imagine what would happen if predators weren't around to eat a bunch of them. They would take over the world."

"The ants didn't bother you?" Blatzo asked.

"Only at first. But they didn't bite, so I got used to it. Letting them crawl over me was worth it. Once you watch the video I took, you'll see."

"I thought you were going to play *Minecraft*," Safdar said.

"I was," Savannah explained as she pulled the twigs out of her hair. "But those little birds kept screeching and screeching. I couldn't concentrate, so I finally climbed the tree to see why they were making so much noise. After that, I couldn't help myself. I mean, you should see how they gobbled the worms and bugs that the mother bird brought. It's right here on the video."

She handed Justine her iPad and told Justine the password to access the video.

They all watched the little birds on Savannah's iPad.

"Way cool," Michael said. "Want to see our fawn video?"

"And my spider building a web?" Safdar said.

"Yes," Savannah said. "I'd like that. A lot."

"Hey, Blatzo," Justine said as she was holding the iPad.

"Don't call me Blatzo," he growled.

"Blatzo," Justine said. "Look, Savannah took a video of us when we stood below the tree."

Justine played the video.

"I hope she's okay. I like her a lot. I wouldn't want her to be lost."

"Yeah. I like her too. She makes me laugh."

"I'm glad she moved to our school. I hope she will sit with us at lunch tomorrow."

"You guys are right. It would be nice if she became a friend."

"I know you guys didn't mean all of that," Savannah said. "But I have to admit, I did like hearing it anyway."

"Actually," Blatzo said, "it was close to the truth."

"Close?" Savannah frowned. Then she grinned. "Well, Blatzo, that's good enough for me."

She gave Blatzo a high five. Then Safdar. Then Justine.

But not Michael. Michael was still looking at the iPad.

"Hey," Michael said. "What's that other video? It looks like me."

He hit *Play*, and all of them could hear Michael's words in the video as he said, "Only one way to find out if it's deer poop."

"Hey!" Michael said. "That's not funny."

"Yes it is," Savannah said. "Especially when I get it up on YouTube."

Savannah grabbed the iPad. And giggled. And ran from Michael as fast as she could.

Chapter Ten

On Earth Day, Justine and Savannah stood in front of the class for their presentation. Mrs. Howie, as usual, sat behind her desk.

"Before Justine and I show our video," Savannah said, "I would like to tell you why I think nature is so amazing. It's a system that works perfectly. There are species that are called producers. Like trees and plants. It's so cool. All they need is sunlight and water to grow and produce edible energy. At the same time, they use up carbon dioxide and produce oxygen."

Savannah didn't need to read from her notes. She was enthusiastic. "Consumers are living beings that eat the producers. As the consumers use energy, they need oxygen, but they produce carbon dioxide.

Isn't that amazing? That the waste from consumers is fuel for producers and vice versa?"

Savannah didn't stop there. "The third group is the decomposers. Like bacteria that go to work when an animal or plant dies, or break down animal waste products like poop. The decomposers make the soil rich with nutrients to support the producers. And the producers support the consumers. And the consumers support the decomposers. It's called an ecosystem. The ecosystem is an amazing chain of interactions that will blow your mind if you stop and think about how it works. I was proud to help count species and send my numbers in to the scientists."

"Yes," Justine said. "But if any part of the chain is hurt by pollution or anything else, it can destroy the entire balance."

Justine looked at Mrs. Howie. "You told us our assignment was to show why we should care about the environment. Although it saves resources and

it can save money to reduce, reuse and recycle, I finally understand why I want to be the Queen of Green."

Savannah jumped in. "And I really want to become green, so that's why I want to be called the Queen of Mean to Be Green."

"Yes," Justine said. "We have the answer to your question, Mrs. Howie. Would you mind if we turned the lights down and let the class watch a video?"

"Not at all," Mrs. Howie said.

The video began. Savannah and Justine had created it using footage from their trip into the woods. It began with the fawn that Michael and Blatzo had found. Then it flashed to the spider Safdar had captured building a web. Savannah's video of the baby birds in their nest came next, followed by footage of frogs from another one of Justine's trips into the woods. The video ended with a slow-motion shot of a flower opening up to sunlight. They had added music to the video and edited it carefully. It was so beautiful that when it finished, everyone in the class stood up and cheered.

"Do we need to say more about why we should all want to be green?" Justine asked.

"No," Mrs. Howie answered. "The ecosystem truly is amazing. Let's work together to keep it that way."

"Thank you," Savannah said. "But there is one last thing the class needs to learn about nature."

"What's that?" Mrs. Howie asked.

"I would like to answer that by showing one last video," Savannah said. "Watch closely."

The video showed Michael as he reached down and scooped up some dark pellets.

"Only one way to find out if it's deer poop," Michael said in the video. The class watched as Michael popped the dark pellets into his mouth. "You taste them."

The class laughed and laughed as the video showed Michael spitting and wiping his tongue with both hands. Michael laughed the loudest.

"Yes," Savannah said as the video ended, "when you enjoy nature, it's very, very important to never, ever eat deer poop. Leave that job to the decomposers."

JUSTINE McKEEN
vs. the QUEEN of MEAN

Notes for Students and Teachers

Become a Science Observer and help the global environment!

As a student or teacher, you really can make a difference in the science world! (And have fun. And spend little to no money on your project.) Technically, the term is called *crowd sourcing*.

This is the practice of combining the efforts of a large group of contributors. For scientists, this means collecting information from dozens, hundreds or even thousands of participants to give them a big-picture idea of what is happening in the environment.

There are lots of different environmental areas in which you can do scientific research as individuals or as a classroom. Below are a few suggested apps for your iPhone or Android as well as websites that you can use to become involved.

Enjoy!

Apps for Science Observers

Project Noah—a free app for iPhone or Android

A tool for nature enthusiasts who want to explore and document wildlife.

www.projectnoah.org/

What's Invasive—a free app for iPhone or Android

An app that displays local lists of invasive plants or animals.

www.whatsinvasive.org

Marine Debris Tracker—a free app for iPhone or Android

Users can find and log marine debris on beaches or in the water.

www.marinedebris.engr.uga.edu

Creek Watch—a free app for iPhone
Designed to help citizen scientists monitor the health of their local watershed.

http://creekwatch.researchlabs.ibm.com/

Websites for Science Observers

Plant Watching

www.budburst.org

Frog Watching

www.aza.org/frogwatch/

Ant Watching

http://schoolofants.org

Spider Watching, Roadkill Project and More

www.scistarter.com

Enter keyword (spider, roadkill, etc.) into the search bar to find a project that interests you!

Sigmund Brouwer is the bestselling author of many books for children and young adults, including the popular Justine McKeen, Queen of Green series. *Justine McKeen vs. the Queen of Mean* is the sixth book in the series. Sigmund lives in Red Deer, Alberta, and Nashville, Tennessee. For more information, visit www.rockandroll-literacy.com.